World of Readin

STAR WARS.
GALAXY OF ADVENTURES

EROES & VILLAINS

WRITTEN BY ELLA PATRICK
ART BY TITMOUSE

DISNEY
LUCASFILM
P R E S S

LOS ANGELES · NEW YORK

Printed in the United States of America

First Edition, September 2019   10 9 8 7 6 5 4 3 2 1

Library of Congress Control Number on file

FAC-029261-19221

ISBN 978-1-368-04556-8

Visit the official *Star Wars* website at: www.starwars.com.

SUSTAINAB[E] FORESTRY INITIATIVE

Certified Sourcing

www.sfiprogram.org
SFI-01415

There are many heroes and
villains in the *Star Wars* galaxy.
A hero is someone who helps others
so there can be peace.
Peace is when there is no fighting.

The Jedi are a group of heroes
in the galaxy.
The Jedi use the Force
and lightsabers to protect others.

The Force is an energy field
that connects all living things.
Lightsabers are swords
made of light.
Lightsabers can be
all different colors.

Yoda is a very wise Jedi.
Yoda is small and green,
and he is very strong.
Yoda teaches others
how to become Jedi.

Luke Skywalker lived on a farm.
But now he is learning
how to be a Jedi.

Luke wants to help

protect the galaxy.

Luke needs to protect the galaxy
from the villain Darth Vader.
Darth Vader used to be a Jedi
named Anakin Skywalker.
But he fell to the
dark side of the Force.

Darth Vader is evil.

He uses a red lightsaber.

Darth Vader wants to rule the galaxy with the evil Emperor.

The Emperor is the leader
of the Galactic Empire.
He is strong in the
dark side of the Force.
He can shoot lightning
out of his hands.

Soldiers who fight for the Empire
are called stormtroopers.
Stormtroopers wear matching
white armor and helmets.

The rebels fight
against the Empire.
Princess Leia helps lead
the rebels.

Leia is smart and brave.

She is not afraid of the Empire.

Leia is also kind.

Like Luke, Leia wants to bring
peace to the galaxy.

Luke and Leia are not alone.

They have friends to help them.

C-3PO and R2-D2 are droids.

Droids are robots.

C-3PO is tall and gold.

R2-D2 is short and blue.

C-3PO is often scared.

R2-D2 is not.

R2-D2 talks in boops and beeps.

Han Solo and Chewbacca the Wookiee
are brave pilots and good friends.
Han and Chewie fly a fast ship
called the *Millennium Falcon*.

Sometimes the rebels fight
the Empire in big space battles.

Rebel pilots fly ships
called X-wings.
R2-D2 helps Luke fly
an X-wing in battle.
X-wings fire red laser blasts.

Imperial pilots fly black ships
called TIE fighters.

TIE fighters scream through space
and fire green laser blasts.

The Empire also has massive ships
called Star Destroyers.
Star Destroyers have
powerful laser cannons.

Star Destroyers carry
stormtroopers, TIE fighters,
and other ships inside of them.

Sometimes the rebels fight
the Empire on the ground,
like on the ice planet Hoth.

The Empire's heavy AT-AT walkers

stomp across the battlefield.

The rebel snowspeeders

use tow cables to tie up

the AT-AT's legs.

And sometimes these heroes and villains fight with lightsabers.

The rebels will not stop fighting
until the Empire is defeated.
In the *Star Wars* galaxy,
every day is an adventure!